To the memory of my grandmother, Julia Macrae – J.D.

And for my grandmother, Ganga – C.V.

PUFFIN BOOKS
UK | USA | Canada | Ireland | Australia | India | New Zealand | South Africa
Puffin Books is part of the Penguin Random House group of companies
whose addresses can be found at global.penguinrandomhouse.com.
www.penguin.co.uk   www.puffin.co.uk   www.ladybird.co.uk

 Penguin
Random House
UK

First published 2013
First published in this edition 2017
002
Text copyright © Julia Donaldson, 2013
Illustrations copyright © Charlotte Voake, 2013
The moral right of the author and illustrator has been asserted
Made and printed in China
A CIP catalogue record for this book is available from the British Library
ISBN: 978–0–141–37827–5

MIX
Paper from
responsible sources
FSC
www.fsc.org
FSC® C018179

The Further Adventures of
The Owl
and the
Pussy-cat

Julia
DONALDSON

PUFFIN

Charlotte
VOAKE

The Owl and the Pussy-cat went to sleep
By the light of the moon so pale.
Their beautiful ring was tied with string
In a bow round the Pussy-cat's tail.

They dreamed of mice, and raspberry ice,
  While slumbering cheek to cheek.

But down flew a crow who unravelled the bow
  And flew off with the ring in his beak,
    His beak, his beak,
  And flew off with the ring in his beak.

The Owl and the Pussy-cat woke next day
To find that their ring had gone.
They wept in the shade of the Bong-tree glade
Where never the sun had shone.

The Owl sang songs of terrible wrongs
    While Puss blew her nose on a leaf.

Then she said with a yowl, "O lugubrious Owl,
    Let us travel in search of the thief,
        The thief, the thief,
    Let us travel in search of the thief."

The Owl and the Pussy-cat sailed away
In a beautiful blue balloon.
They took some jam, and a honey-roast ham,
Which they ate with their runcible spoon.

They sought the ring from autumn to spring,
    Till they came to the Chankly Bore.

And there stood the crow, with his head hanging low,
    Shedding tears on the silvery shore,
        The shore, the shore,
    Shedding tears on the silvery shore.

"*Alas and alack,*" said that bird so black,
 "'Tis I who have caused your woes.
 I fear I have sold your ring of gold
 To the Pobble who has no toes."

So they crossed the sea, and the Jelly Bo Lee,
   To the Pobble's improbable land.

And there he sat, with his Aunt and her Cat,
   And they spotted their ring on his hand,
      His hand, his hand,
   And they spotted their ring on his hand.

"*Dear friends*," said the Pobble. "You see how I hobble,
  For all of my toes have gone,
Yet my fingers are fine, and this ring is divine.
  O do let me keep it on!"

Said the Owl, "Too-whoo!" and with Pussy he flew,
To visit the Calico Doves,

Who flapped in the air, while they knitted a pair
Of impeccable gossamer gloves,
Two gloves, two gloves,
Two impeccable gossamer gloves.

The Owl and the Pussy-cat showed the gloves
   To the Pobble who has no toes,
And both of them fitted, so well were they knitted,
   In stripes of magenta and rose.

"*I* am quite in love with the right-hand glove,
    And the left is a joy to behold."

He clapped and he hopped, and he willingly swapped
    The gloves for the ring of bright gold,
        Bright gold, bright gold,
    The gloves for the ring of bright gold.

The Owl and the Pussy-cat sailed back home
To the land where the Bong-tree grows.
They dined on stew with the Jumbly crew
And the Dong with the luminous nose.

They danced a jig with the Turkey and Pig,
  Then sang to the Owl's guitar,

"O dearest love, by the stars up above,
  How delightfully happy we are,
    We are, we are,
  How delightfully happy we are."